BLACK-EYED
SUSAN

BLACK-EYED SUSAN

A NOVEL

by

JENNIFER ARMSTRONG

Illustrated by

EMILY MARTINDALE

Crown Publishers, Inc. • New York

Published by Crown Publishers, Inc., a Random House company,
201 East 50th Street, New York, New York 10022

CROWN is a trademark of Crown Publishers, Inc.

Manufactured in the United States of America

Library of Congress Cataloging-in-Publication Data
Armstrong, Jennifer, 1961–
Black-eyed Susan / by Jennifer Armstrong.
p. cm.
Summary: Ten-year-old Susie and her father love living on the South
Dakota prairie with its vast, uninterrupted views of land and sky, but
Susie's mother greatly misses their old life in Ohio.
[1. Frontier and pioneer life—Fiction. 2. Parent and child—Fiction.
3. South Dakota—Fiction.] I. Title.
PZ7.A73367B1   1995
[Fic]—dc20   95-2276

ISBN 0-517-70107-3 (trade)
0-517-70108-1 (lib. bdg.)

10 9 8 7 6 5 4 3 2 1   First Edition

BLACK-EYED SUSAN

THE PRAIRIE

ONE

The low wind slowed outside our sodhouse door, then rolled over the buffalo grass, bowling down into hollows and up over mounds, blowing the dust before it. I clambered up onto the roof to watch the sun come up, and the wind yanked my pigtails like reins.

"I'm not likely to hup up for the wind," I said to Whitey.

Whitey and Poker were grazing on a little moundy hill nearby, which put them on my level. Whitey nodded as he chewed grass and swiveled one eye at me. He didn't like to hup up for much of anything himself. Even

for a mule, he was stubborn. I plucked a piece of grass of my own, and chewed on it while the sun stretched its arms across the eastern horizon.

Watching the sun rise was a thing I enjoyed doing as often as I could wake up early. The pink and orange and gold went pouring along in both directions, lighting up the land as it went, as though it was making up the golden prairie that very minute, just for enjoyment. One moment all was gray and empty, and the next minute—my lord!—there was the world.

I held my arms wide and turned my palms to the sky. If I squinted so in one direction, it appeared I could touch the horizon on the north and help the sun draw up the land. If I squinted so in the other direction, the same rule applied on the south. I could hold the whole wide plate of the earth between my arms and let the sun come up in the middle.

It always seemed to me that there was a sound that went along with the operation, a deep low tone that the sun made as it rose. But of course there wasn't. One thing the prairie has is silence. I suppose if there *was* a sound, it must have been the wind. The sun rolled its light out onto the world and the wind said, "Now!"

As I say, bringing the sun up was a thing I enjoyed doing, especially in October, when the land was gold.

"Susie! Get off the roof!" my ma called up the chimney. "It's just raining dirt in here!"

The door below me opened and shut, and my pa stepped out into the morning, pulling up his suspenders.

"Come along down, Susie," he said. "We've got a frying pan full of dirt already. Fetch Whitey's bridle, will you, and give it a good oiling this morning."

I shrieked so loud I spooked the mules. They trotted off somewhere out of sight.

6

"Are you riding to town today? Take me, Pa!" I stood up and ran to the edge of the roof.

"Susie!" Ma called again.

I clapped one hand over my mouth. The thought of going to Medicine Fire was so exciting that I could have done a dance. But when you live in a sodhouse, dancing on the roof means a dusty bed and worse.

"Sorry, Ma!" I looked down at Pa. "I hope it wasn't a centipede dropping down on her."

"Come on down here," Pa said, stepping back a bit and holding open his arms. "Don't walk over the roof another step, just take yourself a jump."

The sun was fully up and blazing straight across the prairie into my eyes so I couldn't see my pa's face at all, but I stepped off the edge of the roof anyway. I fell through the dazzle and landed safe in his arms. He caught me and let me slide to the ground. I stood on his feet.

"Pa," I said, reaching up to pull on his beard. "What are you going to town for?"

"One thing and another."

"Is Ma going, too?"

Pa winced his eyes a bit. "I don't know that she will. She's feeling low."

"I noticed that."

I looked over my shoulder at the door. A sodhouse is a cross between a brick house and rabbit hole, in that it is built up with walls but the bricks are just big squares of sod cut right from the ground and stacked up high. The result is a pretty tight burrow against the wind, and if you choose to, you can graze your livestock on the roof as long as you build into the side of a moundy hill.

But my ma grew up in Ohio, and she was used to a more regular style of house, and to a less persistent sort of wind. Also, I expect, she was used to fewer bugs in the ceiling. And as they say, a sodbusting farmer prays for rain, but a sodbuster's wife prays for dry:

if it rains two days outside, it'll rain four days in.

The door was shut, even though the sunlight was washing up against it like spring flood. I pictured the wooden houses in town. From the outside, they appeared to be free of dirt and fairly dry. I looked at Pa again.

"Are we likely to build our wooden house next year?"

We went around the house to scout the mules. "It's a possibility, though remote," he replied. "I'm intending to put our money into buying another quarter section of land. I intend to visit the Land Office today."

We walked through the grass, and with each step we took, grasshoppers sprang into the air and disappeared on the wind. I took Pa's hand, and we climbed up the little hill behind the house. Whitey and Poker were down behind it, where it was still dim and daybreaky.

From where we stood with the sun at our

backs, all of the Dakotas swept out west ahead of us. The land was flat overall, but rippled and wrinkled and rumpled as a morning blanket. The tops of the dried grasses bent away from us in the cold wind, and our shadows pointed long and straight into the farthest distance.

I'd seen maps of the Dakota Territory with each 160-acre section as neat and rectangular as a page from a Bible. But the prairie didn't lend itself to such order when you looked at it in the sunrise. It didn't have the look of something you could boss around at all.

"We should have kept on going," Pa said in his faraway voice. "We would have hit the mountains, and your ma would have had some trees to look at."

I regarded him, and then our west-pointing shadows where they stretched out across the land. There wasn't a tree within twenty miles of us, just some twisty box elders and cottonwoods along the creek out-side of Medicine Fire.

"I don't find trees much to look at," I mentioned. "To my mind, they seem rude, like a person standing in the way of a fine view."

Pa laughed, and the mules switched their ears our way. "That's not everyone's opin-ion," he said. "And I expect you'll have to get a different notion before long whether you care to or not. The trees are coming after us."

I looked back over my shoulder. There was not a thing in sight but our house, and our wagon and lean-to shed, and the wide, wide acres of golden wheat stubble with the black dirt between. If any trees were advanc-ing on us, they were surely sly.

Pa noticed me looking. "They're slow, honey. But all the time that people push west across the plains, they plant trees where they settle, to remind them of home."

"Like pulling the trees after them."

"I suppose so."

We stood in the wind some more, watching our shadows on the shaking prairie grass. The mules chewed, and raised their heads to glance around, and chewed some more. I tried to place a few trees here and there in my mind's eye. I couldn't quite do it.

"Are you going to get Ma a tree today?"

Pa scratched his neck. "It's late in the year for planting trees."

I looked over the prairie, where nothing stirred except the wind, and then took a look at Pa.

He must have seen some misgiving in my face. "I don't think your view would suffer from having one or two trees," he said. "They might set it off, and make the prospect that much finer by contrast."

"Well, I guess that could be so, Pa."

He laughed again. "You're a purist, Susie. Now let's get the mules."

TWO

When I went into the house to see about breakfast, I found Ma sitting up in the bed in the corner, reading a book she'd read many times over the years, *Mansfield Park*, which she had informed me is about people in a big house in England, Europe. I set Whitey's bridle on the table, and opened the crock where we kept our cornmeal. Ma didn't say anything.

"I could make some cornbread," I offered.

"That's a welcome suggestion." Ma was reading hard and didn't look up. The lamp beside the bed was smoking a little, too, but she didn't take notice of that either.

Although the iron stove was warm, it was not hot enough for baking or making coffee. We burned dried animal droppings, wood being so scarce, and I must say a dry mule-ball didn't make much of a fire. I stoked the stove some, trying not to rattle the poker too loud and disturb my ma, and then mixed up some batter and poured it in a pan. When I did that, I noticed a pile of letters on the table ready to go to the post office, all letters Ma had written to her brothers and sisters back in Ohio. I never asked what she wrote to them about, as it didn't seem right to pry. But it gave me a left-out feeling to see how many letters she had written. I glanced at Ma, but she was miles away. It was awfully lonesome inside the house.

I had to clear my throat before I could talk. "Does that book have trees in it?"

Ma marked her place with one finger and looked up, and a smile slowly spread across her face. "Yes, it does. Lots of trees." She

looked at me for a bit in a considering way, and then set the book down and held back the blankets. "Come on in here, Susie."

In a blink, I kicked off my shoes and climbed into the bed beside Ma, where it was warm. She snugged the covers around us both and put my head against her shoulder.

"It's a beautiful day," I told her. "The sky is as blue as anything."

"Hmm." She stroked my arm. "Is the wind blowing?"

"Yes, ma'am."

"Then let's not discuss it, if you please."

"Yes, ma'am." I pressed my cheek against her shoulder, wishing I could think of a way to get my ma out of the house. She'd hardly stepped foot outside in weeks, now.

I couldn't bring to mind when it had started, that lonesomeness of hers. Maybe it had been there from the time we settled our homestead, when I was five, and I just hadn't noticed it before. Perhaps it had been growing like a seed, and was blooming at last with a pale flower and a sad perfume. All I knew was that Ma never laughed anymore, hardly spoke, seldom smiled. From time to time, I wondered if she would ever feel like being my ma again. Rumor was a Bohemian woman had walked away from her family's claim one day last winter and not come back. I didn't worry about my ma wandering off, since she hated to go outside. But I did worry about her going into that book of hers sometime and not coming out again.

"I was lying here remembering something this morning," she said as she snugged me in tighter. "It strikes me that it must be one of my earliest memories."

Her small smile cheered me up a degree. "Are you going to tell me it?"

"Of course." Ma hugged me a bit, and then settled in for storytelling.

"When I was a small child, my mother

had a regular washday, when a hired girl came to help her wash all the sheets and the tablecloths, and they'd hang out on the line, swaying so gently when a breeze came, like old ladies in white dresses, dancing slow. They'd hang out there all day as long as it was fine, just drying and gathering up a nice smell.

"Then, on the following day, my mother would iron them all, and I would hide under the ironing board while my mother pressed. The sheets would drape down on both sides at the ends of the board like a tent, and I'd crawl in under there to hide. It was always warm and steamy and smelled of starch, and the light was white and soft, like being in a cloud.

"My mother liked to recite Shakespeare when she ironed, although I didn't know at the time what she was saying. I only knew it made a lovely sound. And the iron would thump-thump, thump-thump over my head like a beating heart, and I could hear my mother's voice not talking to me but knowing I was there. No one could see me, hidden under the ironing board."

Ma stopped talking, and she let out a sigh. I looked up at her, past the one big braid that came down over her shoulder and tickled my nose. Beyond her head, sheets were nailed into the walls and ceiling to keep the dirt from falling into the bed. My ma still looked miles away.

"I'm sorry I'm such bad company for you, Susie," Ma said, pleating the bedspread with her fingers. "I shouldn't let you make breakfast while I lie here feeling sorry for myself."

I had to swallow hard. My throat was tight. "I don't mind it, Ma."

"Well," she said in a brisk and hopeful voice. "I should get up, anyhow. This is a farm, not a manor house."

She shoved the covers back in one fast sweep, and shooed me out of bed. Her night dress was as white as the sheets, and her face was very white, too. We both wriggled our toes into our shoes. Ma rested one hand on my shoulder.

"Are you going to ride to town with Pa, today?" she asked me. Her eyes were gray and kind, as always, but I was worried that she might still be lonesome.

"Not if you don't want me to, Ma."

"No, of course not. Go ahead and have some fun," she said.

I put my arms around her waist. "You come too, Ma. I'll ride with Pa on Whitey, and you can come on Poker. Or we'll take the wagon." I tipped my head back to look up at her, and my heart beat hard. "Say yes, Ma. It's a fine day for riding. Pa says you used to be a real fine horsewoman."

She smoothed my hair back and let my braids slip through her hands. "No, Susie. I'll stay here. I'll stay inside."

I hung my head, and she walked to the

stove to check on the cornbread, hitching a blanket around her shoulders as she stooped to the job. And then Pa came in, and he began to talk about what he intended to do in Medicine Fire, and I didn't add anything more to the conversation. It wasn't much of a conversation, anyway, as it was mostly Pa speaking, and waiting for Ma to say something in reply. For the most part she didn't contribute much from her side, and I could hear that sound in Pa's voice that meant he was in a struggle to keep talking himself.

I ate my cornbread and worked some lard into Whitey's bridle so that it'd get well seasoned. By doing both at once, I managed to cover my hands and Whitey's bridle equally in lard and cornbread crumbs. But I knew Whitey wasn't exactly a proud animal, and was in no position to object.

Since my folks were still having their conversation, such as it was, I took myself outside, just to see how the day was coming along, and if the truth be told, to see if that wouldn't be a hint to my Pa to hurry up.

Then a piece of fire appeared to skim by my vision. I spun around, and it was an orange butterfly.

"Hold on there," I cried, and dropped the bridle and lit out after the monarch.

For such a fragile thing, it was capable of some speed. I chased it, and it continually fluttered up out of reach, and then settled down like it was resting. Then I'd sneak up on it, ready to make a grab, and off it'd go in another direction altogether, with me in pursuit. I ran after it, through long grass and crickets, until I could scarcely breathe. It fluttered on its way as if it had never noticed me at all.

"Have a good trip!"

I stood there, and the wind moved through the long grass like a dog sniffing for flickertails. And then I heard a whistle—

seet!—and that was a flickertail. So I ran in that direction to see if I couldn't spot the hole before the gopher disappeared.

Seet! from behind me and I ran off that way, and *seet!* to the right, like some invisible trickster flickertail that only wanted to bedevil me.

Seet!

"I give up!" I laughed, wiping my brow. "I'm not having any luck catching things today."

As I stood there collecting my breath, the grass made a whispering sound as if to say— *Take a look*. And there I found myself, out on Buffalo Ridge, with nothing but prairie on every side. I turned around again, trying to place myself.

In times of consideration, I like to sit and consider. So that is what I did. I sat down.

Up above me, the tops of the grasses leaned over like a crowd of mourners glooming into a grave, and beyond their heads was the wide blue sky. I pictured my ma sitting at the table with her hands clutched in her lap, or standing by the photograph of her sisters and brothers on the porch of that fine house in Ohio with the picnic table set up under the trees, and I thought to myself how close to destroyed she'd be if I got lost out on the prairie. I took in one long, slow breath to show myself how I wasn't at all scared about getting misplaced. I had to do it again, and then I made to stand up.

And then a glimmer of paleness caught my attention. I parted the grass with my hands and beheld a buffalo skull, staring dead and white, with a little spiderweb in one eye and a tuft of grass sprouting from the other. It was a large example of skull.

"First-rate!" I crowed.

I dragged it toward me with considerable effort. It wasn't often you got to find such big bones, and they were worth a good sum of money. Factories back east were grinding them up into powder to use for some process or other, and most homesteaders had a good pile of bones stored up to haul to the depot. People say these prairies used to be thick with buffalo, herds so big you could ride through them for a hundred miles, with a cloud of dust rolling along that hid the sun for days.

What they say about those herds might be a stretcher or it might not. In all my life, all ten years, I had not met a single buffalo myself. But if it was true, then it seemed like the buffalo had come a long way down. They'd gone from clouds of dust to a pile of fine white powder in a pretty short space of time. Ashes to ashes, they say. Dust to dust. Nothing lasts long on the prairie before it gets blown away and the wind brings along something to take its place.

I dragged the skull another foot, and then I stood on top of it. A buffalo skull is a large item, and it gave me enough of a boost so I could see a ways farther on. I spied Pa, small in the distance.

I made such a racket of shrieking and hollering that he eventually heard me. He turned and held one hand out from his brow to spot me out in the grass, and then gave me a big wide wave. He started walking my way, so I sat down on the skull to wait. After not too long a time, I heard the shush-shush of grass against his striding legs. His head was the first thing I saw coming toward me.

"What are you doing out here?"

"Farming," I said in a proud manner. I jumped up so he could see what fruits of the earth I'd reaped.

"A prime specimen," Pa said, hunkering down to look at it face-to-face. He pulled the spiderweb out of the eye socket and wiped it on his knee, and he tipped the skull this way and that to look it over. "We ought to get some good credit for this at the Mercantile."

I gazed down at the skull. "Maybe we could trade it for a tree. That'd cheer Ma."

He eyed me. "I believe it's going to take more than a tree."

"Pa?"

"Yes, missy?"

The lonesome wind blew some wispy hair into my face and whispered "how" in my ears. "How come Ma won't bake pies anymore? Don't you remember she used to make pies?"

For a moment he didn't answer. He was looking down at the buffalo skull, and I thought for a moment he hadn't exactly heard me.

"Pa? She used to make pies and cut out crust on the top to make it look like a flower, all goldeny piecrust petals with a black hole in the middle, remember?"

"I remember. She just doesn't want to make them, I guess."

He dragged the skull up and hefted it into

his arms. "Let's go. We're taking the wagon and it's ready."

With Pa I knew I could find the way. I ran on ahead, huffing and puffing, and soon spotted our house. The team was hitched and the mules were switching their tails. Just as I approached, the door opened and Ma came out, clutching a blanket around her, her eyes wide.

"Susie! Where were you? Where'd you go?"

"Just around, Ma," I brought out.

She clutched me to her, driving her fingers hard into my shoulders. "You could get lost! Don't wander!"

My face was mashed against her body. I felt terrible about causing her grief, but I couldn't breathe. "Ma!" I pushed away from her. "I wander all the time. And I found something good this time."

"What?"

Pa came striding up, and I felt I'd made quite an accomplishment. "Look at that skull, Ma!" I cried as he set it down at her feet. "Isn't that a sight?"

She took one look at that old death's-head and turned a shade whiter than the skull. Without another word, she turned and went back into the house. Pa and I stood in silence for a moment, and the wind tossed a little dust into my eyes. Poker rattled his harness.

"Ma's not in a mood to appreciate bones, it seems," I said, blinking hard.

"So it seems." Pa picked up the skull again and took it to the wagon. I popped open the door of the house.

"Ma, we're leaving," I called.

She was lying on the bed, her back to the room.

"Want anything from Medicine Fire?" It was hard to look at her back, all stiff and miserable. I fiddled with the door latch.

"Not one blessed thing," she replied in a muffled voice.

"Ma, I don't suppose you could make a pie for dinner? I'd love a pie."

She shook her head. "Not today, Susie. I don't have a pie in me today."

I closed the door quietly and pulled myself up into the wagon. Pa didn't speak. He hupped the mules, and we started out with a jerk, the wheels dipping and bumping in the track.

"Hup, Whitey, you lazy old cuss. Hup, Whitey." Pa kept up a continuous scold to keep Whitey from hanging back in the harness and making Poker do all the work. On either side of us, the empty prairie stretched on into the ends of forever. And behind us, Ma inside the sodhouse got farther and farther away.

THREE

Whitey was lagging. Pa kept a scatter of pebbles in the wagon, and from time to time he clipped one at Whitey's rump. The mule would look sharp and walk smart for a while, but then he'd ease up on the harness again. Poker plodded along, his heavy head going up and down, as though he had seen enough horizon to satisfy him for a lifetime and wasn't planning to look at it ever again.

"It's nice to see so far, don't you believe so, Pa?" I asked.

Pa drove, resting his elbows on his knees.

He squinted his fine blue eyes around at the wide, wide prairie. "Nicest thing there is, I believe."

"And you wouldn't want any old trees, would you?"

"No, miss, I myself could get along fine without them." Pa handed me the reins. "Like to drive?"

"Would I!" I sat up straight and gave Whitey a warning. "Don't you go trying anything tricksy on me! I'm watching."

Pa leaned against the backrest and the sun sat on his shoulders like the epaulets of a general's uniform. He was a tall, handsome man, in my opinion, and anyone could see he'd gone soldiering in his younger days. The Civil War, it was. A number of the American men in Dakota Territory had taken some part in that fight before they settled out on the prairie. As for the European homesteaders, they might have had their own wars back home, as far as I knew.

"Pa. Tell me more about that war you were in."

"That's a long time ago. Long ago."

"Before I was born, right?" I held the reins high and light, wanting to show how well I could manage, and I slid a glance his way. The whole sky stood behind his head.

He nodded slowly. "Before you were born, honey. I fought for President Grant when he was General Grant. I followed him all over the states of Virginia and Pennsylvania, which if I never see again, I'll die a happy man."

"What are they like? Like this?" I indicated the few hundred acres or so in our immediate vicinity. The wagon road was two ruts across the golden spread of grass that rose slow ahead of us; the ruts appeared to come out of Whitey's head between his ears and move on into the distance, and I liked to think that Whitey had no idea how he was creating a road that he had to drag the wagon down. That was fitting justice for an obstinate mule. The roads ran straight as a beam of light out there: they followed section lines, the borders of homesteads that had checkerboarded the prairie. A hawk of some variety cut across the line of the road at a slant, caring not a bit for the geometry of the mapmakers. Pa and I followed the bird's progress until it grew so small it disappeared into the sky. A wind passed in front of us, and we could watch its progress too as it pushed grass and traveled on. The quiet was immense.

"Those places are not like this," Pa said. "You can't see so far."

I kept quiet and waited. I chucked a little rock at Whitey just to keep the action going.

"There was one fight they call the Battle of the Wilderness," Pa said. He frowned at the horizon, almost as though he'd like to push it out even farther.

"There's a river called the Rapidan comes

running out of the Blue Ridge Mountains up near the top of Virginia. It's a pretty river, and it was a pretty time of year, early in May. The trees were leafed out, making the whole countryside that pretty pale green up the hillsides and all around, little lookout hills called Pony Mountain and Clark's Mountain. I recall there were lilacs blooming, which perfumed the air, and real early in the morning the red-winged blackbirds by the banks of the river would set up their whistling and calling. A fellow in my regiment shot a woodcock, and about six of us had a taste when it was cooked.

"That was the last food I ate for two days. The Wilderness was a thick woods, and when the armies of the North and South commenced to fighting, they got tangled up in those woods and you couldn't see the man five feet away from you. The underbrush caught fire, wide sappy rhododendron leaves curling up like fists, fire running up grape vines like they were fuses and setting the treetops ablaze, all those lilac flowers turning to ash. Soldiers shot their comrades in the smoke, and the wounded were burned alive where they lay. You could hear men scream, and horses scream, and you could hear the scream a bullet makes as it goes by your ear. But you couldn't see any of it."

Whitey and Poker both put their ears back at the tone in Pa's voice. I didn't look at him.

"General Grant had a habit of whittling sticks, just whittling away until they disappeared. Many times I saw him do it. That day in the Wilderness I wished we could turn him loose on those woods so he could just whittle it down to nothing. A good number of trees got cut down by cannon fire. But it wasn't enough.

"You couldn't see," Pa repeated. "You couldn't see anything in those woods. Do you understand?"

I gave a look around. On the prairie, all that keeps you from seeing is darkness that comes at last at the end of the day. You can watch a cloud build itself on the horizon and take an hour getting to where you are. Even on a sunless day, there was so much light and brightness that a permanent squint was natural for every homesteader.

"But that's in the past," Pa said, without waiting for an answer. He took the reins from me and gave me a good smile. "Outstanding driving, Susie. I imagine you could handle the team alone."

That pleased me all over and I felt pretty big. But I considered a bit more on Pa's story, and it reminded me of his black-eyed Susans.

Every winter, he ordered seeds for black-eyed Susans from an outfit in Minneapolis. Every spring, he planted them thick on the roof of our sodhouse, and when they bloomed in the summer, you could see our house standing out from the green prairie from just miles away. They're a bright yellow daisy with a big black center, and a crowd of them standing together could take your breath. We'd drive to town more often just so we could watch out for the house on the way back. What a campfire gold they made, like the sun sitting on our roof.

Of course, the wind usually ripped all the petals off in a week or so. But it was a treat for us. Pa would be watching and watching and we'd mount a low rise, and then at once he'd stand on the buckboard and point. "There it is," he'd cry. "What a sight!"

And sure enough, way far in the distance would be our roof of gold.

THE TOWN

ONE

A bull calf was crying in the middle of the street when we drove into Medicine Fire. It put its head down and bawled like anything.

"Lost its ma, I guess," Pa remarked.

"I don't see how a cow could just go and lose her baby." I stretched around in the seat as we passed. Dust from our wheels blew on past the calf and down the street toward Minnesota.

I stretched around the other way. I was trying to look at everything at once, including all the children I saw. There was a girl I knew from when we sometimes went to church. Her name was Lanny. I didn't much like her, but there you go. You can't be too particular when you only see people once in a while.

"Hi, Lanny!" I shouted.

She looked surprised to see me. She ran over to our wagon and trotted alongside, and my angle was such that all I could see of her face below her bonnet brim was her talkity-talking mouth. "Susie, you'll never believe it. There's a piano at the Mercantile now!"

"A real one?"

"As real as you are," Lanny dropped back and waved.

"That girl sure likes to spoil a surprise," Pa said.

"What exactly *is* a piano?" I asked Pa.

"A piano? I guess you haven't seen one yet, have you?"

I felt my eyebrows going way up. "Well, I have *heard* of a piano, Pa. I just never figured out how one works nor ever saw a picture of one. So go ahead and tell me."

"I'm not like Lanny," Pa said with a laugh. "You go into the Mercantile and see for yourself."

"Not yet."

I enjoyed Medicine Fire too much to take it at a rush. For one thing, the street was lined with two- and three-story buildings, which meant you actually had to tip your head and look up at them. Their signs all looked like they'd been scoured with a handful of sand, which I guess they had. Paint doesn't last long when the wind is constantly grinding dust against it. But even so, it was a treat to read the colored letters. The brick store used red paint on its sign, of course, and the undertaker had black. But most of the others had their signs in the same blue and green, leading one to suppose there'd been a lot of that paint going cheap at one time.

Best of all, though, when you let your

gaze sink back to ground level, what did you see but people. Sometimes you'd see as many as ten people on the street at one time, not counting dogs and horses. And each time there was a peek between buildings, there was Little Medicine Creek on one side and the railroad tracks on the other. The town had actual geography, plain as day, with streets laid out all neat and orderly so you could see how the town would grow by and by. Of course, it hadn't grown yet, and all those crisscrossing streets were just lying there on the prairie with no buildings on them; but anyone could tell the town was aiming high and ready for all the folks they expected to step down off the train. I heard hammering and laughing and other sounds of industry from the direction of the grain elevator.

"You look like you're eating something sweet," Pa said, looking down at me with a smile as he turned our team in at the Mercantile.

I hopped down from the wagon and began wrestling the buffalo skull to the back end as Pa hitched the team. "Isn't town fun? I aim to trade this for something to perk up Ma. I'm just sorry she wouldn't come with us."

"Me, too," Pa replied. He dragged the skull out of the wagon and nodded me on ahead of him. "After you, miss."

Over the door of the store was the sign that read "Schirmer's Mercantile and Hardware," in fancy letters which I never grew tired of admiring. I stepped onto the porch and stomped a few times with my feet to hear the hollow wooden sound the planks made. Then I grabbed the two doorknobs with both hands and swung the doors wide, while the bell overhead let out a racket.

"Hello!" I shouted into the dim, dusty store. The wind pushed by me and swept a straw hat right off a counter, just like a clumsy customer, and then went exploring the Mercantile.

Shelves reached up the walls on all sides, filled with such an array it always stopped me in my tracks in wonderment. Bolts of cloth, bins of nails, every size of shoe, boxes of buttons, ready-made clothes, buggy whips, shotguns, peculiar contraptions of a medical and veterinary nature, plow blades, umbrellas, prickly coils of barbed wire, canvas tarps, canning jars, washtubs, Bible stands, wallpaper, oil lamps, sewing machines, hair tonic, fishing tackle, poultry brooders, pig troughs, dinner plates, wigs, corsets, ear trumpets, clocks, anvils, baskets, saws, and who knows what all else sat crowded close together in no particular order, which pleased me fine. And from the ceiling hung a collection of wicker chairs, bicycles, ladders, horse harnesses, wheelbarrows, sled runners, and hayforks, like a flock of the strangest birds in creation, all swaying and rocking as the wind poked around up there. The place smelled of grease, candy, and leather, a very pleasant combination.

Through this crowded Mercantile came Mrs. Schirmer, chins wobbling like a turkey gobbler.

"Susie!" She clasped her hands. "Such a long time has it been. And your papa!"

"Hello, Mrs. Schirmer," my pa said, and shook her hand.

"Papa!" Mrs. Schirmer yelled into the shadows of the store. "Papa, see who it is here!"

She beamed at us as though she'd invented us herself and was well satisfied with the result. "And such a big buffalo skull you are bringing me!"

"I want to trade for a treat for my ma," I told the woman.

"And your mama, how goes it with her?" She was asking me, I guess, but she was looking at Pa.

He didn't answer, and so I thought I should, but then there came Mr. Schirmer stumping out of the backroom, muttering, "What's this? What's this?" Mrs. Schirmer put her hands on my shoulders and turned me to face him.

"See, Papa, how big Susie grows."

Mr. Schirmer stopped and bent down closer to me, his wild bristly eyebrows wiggling around like two caterpillars. He smelled of tobacco.

"This is *not* Susie," he said as he always did.

I nodded and put one hand on my heart. "Honest, I swear, Mr. Schirmer," I said as *I* always did.

"Too big to be Susie—she's only a little thing, like a chicken." He stood up and waved one hand as though shooing flies. "No, I don't believe it."

"I'll prove it to you. *Ein bisschen Zucker, bitte,*" I said, holding my hands out.

He roared with laughter. "She never forgets the German I teach her," he said to Mrs. Schirmer.

We went through this every time I visited the Mercantile, and Mr. Schirmer never grew tired of the routine. I didn't tire of it myself, since it always meant he'd give me a handful of candy—a little sugar, please, just as I'd asked. Of course, he probably handed out free candy to every child within fifty miles of Medicine Fire, not just me. He did once mention that he believed in the power of sweets to correct anything that might be wrong with a youngster, be it rheumatic fever or bad manners. I don't know if he thought I had one of those complaints, but I was happy to take the treats.

I followed him to the display case filled with candy. The glass was smudged with noseprints, and I pressed my nose against it, too, just to be sociable and join the crowd.

"There's a calf out in the street," Pa was telling Mrs. Schirmer.

"*Ach*," she exclaimed, and then hollered at the top of her voice, "Armin! Wolfie! The calf is out again!"

Heavy footsteps pounded out through the back of the store. The Schirmers' four big bachelor sons each had a homestead outside of Medicine Fire, but they all moved back in with their folks after harvest every year. Armin and Wolfie were twins, and younger than Helmut and Karl, but they all looked just exactly alike to me—that is, enormous, blond, red in the face, and so shy they wouldn't open their mouths and give anyone a taste of their voices. Perhaps they figured Mama and Papa Schirmer did all the talking the family was expected to do. They could each of them carry a calf in their arms, and plow or reap for two days without rest, and I once saw one of them punch a green and bucking horse in the head so hard it instantly became the most docile creature in harness leather. Through the windows in the front door I saw one of the twins pick up the calf and carry it off out of sight. Mr. Schirmer grabbed a fistful of cherry suckers and handed them all to me.

"Now, what do you want for that skull?" he asked me.

"Something pretty," I mumbled around a cherry sucker. "Something cheerful."

While Pa recited a list of our needs and wants—ten pounds of salt, thirty pounds of bacon, and so on—and Mrs. Schirmer nodded and said *ja* to each item, Mr. Schirmer ducked under the counter and came back up with something I'd never seen. It was a glass ball full of water, and with a little toy town inside, and pointy green trees and a horse-drawn sleigh.

"This we have just gotten in." Mr. Schirmer shook the ball, and a flurry of white specks inside swirled around like the wildest snowstorm you ever saw. I felt my eyes widen as the snow settled onto the tiny roofs and tiny trees.

"How are you liking that, now?"

"It's the cleverest thing going," I said without hesitation.

"From Bavaria." Mr. Schirmer shook the ball again. "Like me."

I put my eyes right up to the ball to watch the snowstorm. Except for the trees, it was exactly like a Dakota blizzard in there, with snow swirling all around from every direction. Just the last winter we'd had even more blizzards than usual come screaming out of the northwest. During the first one, we heard a mysterious lot of thumping and bumping at the door during the night. Pa allowed as how it might be someone that got caught in it and managed to find our soddy. He lit the lamp and cautioned Ma to get the stove fired up.

But when he carried the lamp and opened the door, what did we find but a little herd of antelope taking shelter from the storm. The lamp shone on a dozen dark eyes in long snow-caked faces, and as shy as those antelope are, they did look as though they'd like to come inside. We stared at them and they stared at us, while the snow came whirling in through the lamplight and the wind made the flame shudder. Then Pa shut the door.

We often heard them out there in the storms that followed, although we never caught a glimpse of them once the weather finally broke. Each time we heard them, Ma became more agitated and wondered out loud if we shouldn't let them in, since it was too brutal outside for any living thing. But Pa always reminded her that they were wild animals, and besides he might want to shoot one for meat sometime. Then Ma would cry out that she wouldn't have our house turned into a trap—that was more brutal than a

Dakota blizzard—and Pa would apologize and promise not to harm them.

And through it all, we'd still hear them huddling against the wall, their trim hooves tapping against the door from time to time and them not knowing we had a gun inside. I guess everyone likes company and society when the elements act mean, even if the prairie is your natural residence, and even if the company you find is as dangerous as the weather.

Two

The bell over the door jing-jangled again while I was looking at the snow-ball. In blew the wind with Mr. Polhemus and Mr. Ford, and all at once the Mercantile seemed to be filled to overbrimming.

"Good thing we got the wheat in on a calm day or our whole crop would've blowed to Chicago, that's all I'll say," Mr. Ford began at a good shout.

"It is not all you'll say and you know it," Mr. Polhemus replied in a low and growly voice.

Mr. Ford slapped his hat against his knee

and held it out like he was begging our attention with it, although he had our attention already. Mr. Ford was a big man with a face like an old saddle that's been out too long, and the voice of a man accustomed to outroaring the wind.

"Now I ask you, why does Polhemus insist I'm a big talker?" he demanded to know. "Mrs. Schirmer, is it right? Is it fair?"

Mr. Polhemus leaned back with his elbows on an incubator. "He's been talking since we met up outside of town. I've been trying to get a word in edgewise for the last five miles. He's been giving me the benefit of his opinion of hogs, not that I asked for it or didn't try my level best to shut him up."

"Pull someone else's leg for a while!" Mr. Ford roared. "That's the untruest thing I ever heard."

Mr. Ford shook hands with Pa and Mr. Schirmer, and then he reached over to my ear, snapped his fingers and there in his palm was one of the cherry suckers.

"How d'you suppose that got in your ear?" he asked me.

I shook my head. Every time I'd ever run into Mr. Ford he'd managed to pull something out of my ear, either a penny or a shiny rock or some such little thing. It was an enduring mystery to me.

"I don't know, but I wish you'd find a gold nugget next time," I said.

Mr. Polhemus looked over the tops of his spectacles at Pa. "Sensible child."

Pa winked at me. "How was your crop, Polhemus?"

"I'll tell you how his crop was," Mr. Ford spoke up. "Better than last year."

"Not that he asked you," Mr. Polhemus said with a long-suffering look at Mr. Ford. "And you don't have to act so all-fired smart about it, since anyone could guess it was good this year compared to last, seeing as how I lost half my last crop to hail."

"But at least you got to use the hail to make ice cream," I reminded Mr. Polhemus.

He glanced at Pa again. "I take back what I said about sensible."

"Well, now," Mr. Ford said, popping one of my cherry suckers in his mouth. "I'm of the opinion that anyone who sees the practical advantage in each and every adversity is bound to be satisfied with life."

"Is there anything you haven't got an opinion about, Ford?" Mr. Polhemus demanded.

"Come, Susie." Mrs. Schirmer shooed me ahead of her like a chicken. "I'll show you what we have that's new."

I heard Pa talk crops with the other farmers, heard them trading weather tales and livestock stories, and then Mr. Ford began to tell his account of the locusts again, a tale that got stranger and more outlandish each time he told it. Not that it wasn't an out-landish tale to begin with, considering how many locusts came the last time. It was a regular biblical plague, with grasshoppers eating everything in sight, including the paint off of signs, the pages out of books, and the green velvet border on Mrs. Kelly's Sunday dress. The farmland looked like a man fresh from the barber—shaved clean. Mr. Ford had told the story so many times he was now claiming to have fought off locusts with a cavalry saber in one hand and the wrath of God in the other. His voice and Pa's laughter followed me and Mrs. Schirmer to the back of the big store.

"Here is our new piano, Susie," Mrs. Schirmer said proudly.

I smacked one hand to my forehead and gaped at the instrument. "That's a piano?"

"Sure. From St. Paul."

I marveled at the thing, all polished and smooth, and with a lacy scarf covering the top. "It's splendid, Mrs. Schirmer. Congratulations."

I stepped back to admire it, and nearly knocked over a dummy in a fancy dress.

"Try it out, Susie," Mrs. Schirmer invited.

I gave her a wary eye. "Meaning what?"

She was smiling from ear to ear. "Go on, try it out." And she leaned over and diddled her fingers across the black and white keys, bringing out a string of notes from inside the case. They flew up into the air of the Mercantile, shooting up among the harnesses and wheelbarrows hanging from the ceiling like they could hitch up and ride away. It staggered me. The tips of my fingers prickled with the echo.

"I knew it made music, but I never expected it would sound like *that*!" I exclaimed when I collected my wits. "This is really a fine piano, Mrs. Schirmer. First one I ever saw, but I'll bet it beats all the others hands down."

She laughed, and pulled a stool over to the instrument, and then took hands to the thing and out poured such a spectacle of beautiful sound I wondered if my heart would keep beating. She could play several notes at once, and those sounds seemed to join together and spring up into the air like angels holding hands and taking flight.

"Do you know the good hymn?" Mrs. Schirmer asked. "In English it says, 'A mighty fortress is our God.'"

I shook my head.

"Ein' feste Burg ist unser Gott," Mrs. Schirmer began to sing, her voice quavery and her eyes lifted to the ceiling, and the music filling up the spaces in the store so that the dim and dusty emporium seemed to grow brighter and brighter by the minute, light just seeming to pour in by the bucket with each verse she sang. I heard Mr. Schirmer add his voice to hers, and I saw the

men had stopped talking and were gathered around behind me. We all stood there like living statues until the hymn finally came to a stop. Even the wind outside was still.

Pa put his hand on my shoulder. "*That's* a piano, Susie."

"I never expected that. I wish Ma could've heard it."

Pa cleared his throat fairly roughly and walked back to the front of the store. I looked at Mrs. Schirmer. "I guess that buffalo skull isn't worth a piano in trade, is it?"

"Not quite, no. I am sorry."

"Too bad, because I think my ma would like this piano."

I stood beside Mrs. Schirmer, not even daring to touch the keys. From behind the door to the Schirmers' parlor, footsteps sounded, and one of those big sons of hers laughed cheerfully and said something I couldn't make out. I heard Mr. Ford and Mr.

Polhemus start arguing again, and Mr. Schirmer read bits from the newspaper to Pa. He was telling about how there was a new building in Chicago all of ten stories tall, and the longest bridge in the world had just opened in Brooklyn, New York, and there was news of all sorts of busy places filled with people and noise and things going on. I felt pretty low all of a sudden.

"Do you suppose they have pianos in Ohio?" I asked Mrs. Schirmer.

"Yes, I'm sure they do, *Liebchen*."

I regarded the floor. It was becoming clear to me that there probably wasn't much of anything I could get for my ma that would cheer her up. If I'd had a boxcar filled with buffalo bones, it still wouldn't be enough. I pictured her laying in her bed, a smoking lamp at her side, the white sheets nailed to the ceiling to keep the dirt off. Nobody could squeeze Ohio into that little sodhouse of ours. Nobody and nothing could accomplish that.

"I guess I'll just take a credit on that skull, Mrs. Schirmer," I said. "I guess I won't buy anything with it today."

THREE

Pa called to me from the front of the store. "Come on, Susie, let's step along."

Mrs. Schirmer caught my hand before I stepped away and looked into my eyes. "You are a good girl, Susie. You can be a help to your mama."

"I don't know how," I managed to say.

She just smiled at me and patted my cheek.

"Bye, Mrs. Schirmer," I said, still feeling low.

I followed Pa out of the Mercantile. He was walking fast, his boot heels loud and echoing on the plank sidewalk. He nodded as we passed two ladies we didn't know, and he tipped his hat to them but didn't slow down any to introduce himself. I didn't speak, as my mind was occupied with thoughts that I couldn't really give voice to. Pa seemed distant himself. I put another cherry sucker in my mouth and held my peace.

We were headed to the Land Office up the street. We had to walk into the wind, and it forced me to keep my head down. I watched my feet walking, and watched the dust that kept blowing around my ankles as I moved. Some horse somewhere was kicking against a stall door, trying to bust out, wanting to go. The animal no doubt didn't realize there wasn't any place *to* go.

"That was a fine hymn," Pa said suddenly in a loud voice.

I stopped to look at him. He was scowling

so fiercely I didn't know what to say. He looked at the Land Office door, grabbed the handle, and shouldered his way in.

Now, Mr. Winchip, the federal land agent, had a sideline in photography. His speciality, as he told anyone who'd listen, was "Natural Art," which most people around Medicine Fire had taken to calling "Winchip Scenes." He'd set up his camera any old place in town or on the prairie and make a photograph of a cloud over the grain elevator, or willow leaves falling into Little Medicine Creek. Nobody could quite make out the point of them, but he claimed to do a good trade in them in Chicago. One of his photographs had been printed in the *Ladies' Home Journal*, and the framed page from that magazine hung on the wall beside the map of all the homestead sections in his part of the Territory.

When Pa and I walked into the Land Office, Winchip was staring at a pile of buckskins and a feathered headdress on his desk, and shaking his head. His expression was a naturally gloomy one. His big box camera and tripod and plate box occupied a corner of the office beside a cold stove.

"Art is a cussed difficult business," he said by way of greeting.

"Hello, Winchip," Pa said, closing the door behind me and crossing to the desk. He fingered the buckskins and raised one eyebrow at the land agent. "Looks like if you had an Indian in these clothes, he evaporated on you."

Winchip snatched the shirt and tossed it to the floor. "Oh, I had a Indian, but he took it into his head to go and leave without a word. I was planning a whole series of photographs," he said with a wild gesture. "'The Proud Warrior.' It was going to be my masterpiece. But now . . ." Winchip looked as mournful as though his dog had died.

"Can't you find another Indian?" I asked,

although I didn't have much idea myself where to find one. I'd only seen two in my whole life, and they were both cavalry scouts.

Winchip folded his arms and looked at me crossly. "I ain't about to go chasing Indians around the Black Hills, which is where the Sioux mostly all are these days."

"Why not choose a different subject to photograph?" Pa asked. He looked fairly skeptical of the operation. "How about 'The Loud Wheat Farmer'? We've got plenty of those."

Winchip spoke in a voice of rising anger. "You don't understand! Indians are real popular back East. Real popular. That Buffalo Bill Cody's got himself a 'Wild West Show' he's touring all over New York and Baltimore and Philadelphia and them places. He's actually got Sitting Bull in his show— *Sitting Bull,*" he repeated furiously. "And I ain't got even one sorry specimen to take a photograph of. There's money to be made, and I'm missing the train again. Wouldn't even have to be a real Sioux—heck, those folks back East don't know the difference. They just like the costuming and gadgetry."

"Sorry I can't produce one for you, Winchip," Pa said in a running-out-of-patience voice.

"Well, that's that." Winchip wore a look of disgust. "Figures it's still Indians giving me a pain. When I first came out here everyone was sure the Sioux would massacre their families and steal their stock. Now we finally got rid of them and who's suffering again? Winchip."

I had used to like Mr. Winchip, and I certainly enjoyed his Winchip Scenes, but he was beginning to give *me* a pain. I tugged on Pa's sleeve.

"Can I say something, Pa?" I whispered.

Pa looked down at me, maybe a little startled to find me still there. "Sure, honey."

I tugged his sleeve again and jerked my head toward the door. "Out there?"

Mr. Winchip instantly busied himself with papers and maps, sweeping the Indian costume off his desk with his arm. "Don't mind me, I have plenty of work, I'm a busy man. People coming in here all day long to make claims, one right after the other."

That wasn't true, as was obvious to anyone who'd been standing in the office for ten minutes, like we had. But it wasn't my place to call Winchip a liar, and I had other matters on my mind than the land agent's honesty.

Pa and I stepped outside, where the wind was blowing fresh. "Pa, I don't think we should claim another quarter section."

"What makes you say that?" Pa leaned against the door, folding his arms and regarding me from under his eyebrows.

My thoughts were so much in a twist I started twisting one of my braids in my hand, I couldn't help myself. "Pa, maybe we ought better put the crop money into building a house."

"You know I need it for improving another quarter section," Pa told me. "We file on the parcel next to ours, buy more stock, probably build a barn. It'll take all we made on the harvest this year."

I kept on twisting my braid until it pinched. "I think we ought to live here in Medicine Fire."

"Why, I thought you liked living on the claim!"

"Well, I do, but Ma doesn't, and I just wonder maybe we shouldn't be out there at all."

Pa looked at me in wonder. We neither of us spoke for a minute or so, while the wind pushed against us and the bell on the

Mercantile's door rang faintly. The light was coming from the west now. My shadow copied the way my pinafore was flapping in the wind.

"Seems like we've got no business being out there," I muttered.

"What are you saying, Miss Susie?"

"I don't know."

"You think we should pack up and move somewhere else altogether?" His voice made me wince.

I pictured the prairie from the roof of our sodhouse, saw it spreading out from the center like rays from the sun. And I was shaking my head with bewilderment. It's like that, out there. It's a big place and a big notion, and whenever I tried to do some thinking on the subject, I found it was too big for my head. There isn't a place where you can get high enough to see to the end of the question.

I put my hand into Pa's. "I don't want to leave."

"Nor do I."

"But Ma does."

Pa let out a sigh and shook his head just a bit.

"Well, why'd she ever agree to come out if she was going to be so miserable?"

"She didn't know she'd be so miserable," Pa said. "And besides . . ."

I looked at Pa. "Besides what?" I asked.

"I asked her to."

"And she said yes?"

Pa nodded. "And she said yes." He then made as though he was going to say something more. He opened his mouth, and took a breath, and squinted off at the horizon down the street. But he didn't make any further comment after all. He just turned and went back inside the Land Office to make a claim on the quarter section next to ours.

We weren't going to live in town. I knew that. And I was glad. But I kept twisting my braid, and I felt like crying.

THE ICELANDERS

ONE

We drove out of Medicine Fire with the responsibility of improving another quarter section of land. The U.S. government was generous in giving away acres in the wide unsettled territories, but they made you promise to stay on it for at least five years. We'd kept our side of the bargain on our first quarter section, but now we were starting over again with a new claim. Pa didn't look too pleased about it, but I figured it was his own idea, and anyway, I had a kind of anger against him for the time being and didn't feel very sympathetic.

"Did Ma know you were claiming another

quarter section today?" I asked as Main Street turned to a two-rut track.

Pa slid me a look from underneath a pair of pretty fierce eyebrows. "Yes. What do you take me for, some kind of sneak?"

I didn't want to look at him. I kept my attention on the grasses waving at us from the side of the road. The wind was cutting pretty sharp from the northeast, and I shivered and shrugged my shoulders at the same time.

"Well, miss?"

"No."

The mules plodded along. Their shadows plodded along beside them, stretched-out and long-legged as fine horses swimming in clear water, instead of the stumpy old mules they were. Outside the scratchy silence between me and Pa, there was a whispering of grasses in the wind, soft and hissing like rain into puddles, like Little Medicine Creek slipping around stones, the sound of water moving all around us. You could drown in the silence that the sound made.

Pa was muttering at Whitey, and Whitey kept switching his ears back, first one, then the other, as though he just couldn't believe he was being told to hurry up, it was too much to bear, life was just one long, endless pull without a moment's rest or a gentle word to make the way easy. I took a little look at Pa. I put my hand into his.

"I'm sorry," I told him.

He sighed. "I know you are, honey."

"I just have a bit of worry over Ma," I said, leaning against his knee and looking hard at his profile. There were pale lines at the corners of his eyes where he never tanned, squint lines like white bird's feet. He spent all his days outside working on the land and squinting at the horizon. I touched the top of his cheek where the lines were longest in his dark brown face.

"Ma doesn't have these lines," I said.

He smiled, and that made the lines deepen. His eyes were shiny bright, maybe even with a tear in them. I wasn't sure. The wind was in our faces, which could have accounted for it.

"Your ma is a beautiful woman," he said. "The first time I ever saw her, I told myself: Here is the loveliest person on earth."

I stood on the wagon floor with one arm across Pa's shoulders. That put me just at his level, where I liked to ride, with the same view he had. Whenever the wagon rocked one way or the other, Pa was there, steady as an anchor.

"Where'd you see her first?" I asked.

We shared a look out at the straight road ahead, which drew to a point where the purple sky met the yellow land.

"Mackinac Island, which lies in the Straits of Mackinac, between Lake Michigan and Lake Huron," Pa said as the wagon rocked and swayed through the grass. "There was a fine camp there, a popular place for folks to holiday, and an establishment called the Grand Hotel. I'd been up that way looking for work, but I broke my arm and was just resting up on Mackinac.

"I wasn't staying at that hotel, as it was fancy and expensive, even though they made out it was a camp, with log furniture and plaid blankets. But even if you weren't a guest, anyone who liked could stroll out on the Grand Hotel's veranda, which stretched out so far into the water you could see both lakes from the end of it.

"And one morning I went out there before sun-up, wondering if I could manage a fishing rod with my arm as it was. The water was dark, and mist was smoking along the top of it, and all around were tall dark trees fading back into the dim before dawn, and miles and miles of black and somber lake. Nobody but me was out there so early—at least, I didn't see anyone. But I heard a splash behind me, nothing big, but big enough to make me wonder what it could be.

"So I stood looking down into the water, thinking how dark it was, how deep, when another sound turned my head, and there to my right was a woman rising from the lake, pulling herself up a ladder through the mist. The water poured off of her swimming costume and her hair, making a pool all around her on the veranda, and suddenly the sun was up across Lake Huron and shone on her like she was made of water herself, or diamonds. I was stunned. Just appearing like that, like she'd just been born that second, rising out of the water like an angel of the lake. And she looked at me and smiled and said good morning, and I loved her from that moment."

"And then?"

"We were married by the end of two weeks. Her folks were scandalized: what with her pa being such a bigwig judge back home it didn't seem like good propriety to act so hasty and gypsyish. But she just laughed and told them she insisted they love me for her sake. And since she was the baby of the whole big family and had them all around her little finger, they couldn't refuse her a thing."

Then Pa cleared his throat and said, "Hup, Whitey, step along."

I sat down again beside him with my cheek against his shoulder. The light was growing slant across the whispering grass. "I never knew that story, Pa."

"I never told you it before, that's why."

All around us the grass was waving and moving beneath the wind, shifting and rising and growing dark, and the great sky above us beginning to take on that late-afternoon glow.

"Do you know," Pa went on in a dreamy voice. "Some people say there used to be an ocean here, long ago."

I let out a skeptical sort of laugh. "Pa, I can believe a number of surprising things, but not that."

He laughed, too. "There's many and many a person out here has found fossil fish and seashells in the rocks, the forms of sea creatures turned to stone."

"Honest?" I said, and sat up to look at him squarely.

"Honest." Pa nodded and swept one hand around us in a broad *Behold*. "Instead of grass, water: a whole ocean of water stretching from the Great Lakes to the Rocky Mountains. It's enough to make a man give up wheat and go into fishing."

I was happy as a dog, listening to Pa growing philosophical. We shared the view again, seeing how the land lay about us and fell in swells and rises, the movement of the wind visible in the movement of the grass. I imagined my mother diving into the inland sea at Lake Huron and swimming down in the darkness, swimming west until she pulled herself up out of the depths into the bright sky of the Dakotas, rising up and sparkling like crystal. I imagined her turning with a smile, smiling at me and holding out her hand and saying, "Good morning, Black-Eyed Susan."

It wasn't all that hard, really, to think of it as water, and us voyaging across it. I actually stood up, watching for a sail.

And far ahead of us, cresting the top of one swell in the road was the white canvas of a prairie schooner, beating into the wind.

TWO

"Let's catch them up." Pa gave a smart yell at the mules, and Whitey and Poker actually broke into a trot. The wheels clickety-clicked beneath us, and our shadows rippled along the rippling grass beside us. As we got closer we could make out that the other wagon was pulled by two creamy oxen, and the faint sound of the bells around the cattle's necks came to us against the wind.

"How far do you suppose they're going?" I asked Pa.

"Who can say? All the way to Oregon Territory, perhaps, or just to the end of this next mile."

Our wagon seemed not to move, as though we ran in place with the whole silent weight of the sky holding us down, and every blade of grass and bump of land just like every other. But bit by bit, the tinkling bells got louder, and at last they came within shouting distance. From underneath the canvas at the back of their wagon, one little head peeked out and then popped back inside again. We bumped over the rough edge of the road to draw up beside the drivers—a man and a woman.

"Hello!" Pa called, standing up and taking off his hat. "Where are you headed?"

"Vest," the man replied.

"Better come spend the night with us, then," Pa said, and hupped the mules to get ahead of them.

"Tanks!" the man shouted.

I clambered back over the seat, over the sacks of flour and bacon and salt, to the very back of the wagon. The pioneers' oxen were just before my face, long-lashed and smiley-looking.

"Hello," I said to the couple doing the driving. "Heading out to Oregon or Washington Territory?"

"Not so far," the woman replied. "Ve tink Montana."

The man and woman both had blond hair, the woman with braids coiled around the top of her head and the man with a bushy red beard. And between her round right shoulder and the man's lean left was another blond head: a boy, about my size. He looked at me, and climbed out onto the seat between his folks. His hair was so blond it was white.

"I'm Siggi Eiriksson," he told me, pointing at his chest. "I speak the best English from all of us."

"Ask them where they're from," came Pa's voice from the front of our wagon.

"Where are you folks from?" I asked,

sitting on a side of bacon. It smelled nice and smoky, and I bounced along on top of it as though the old pig itself was giving me a ride.

"First from Iceland," Siggi answered. His eyes widened. "Was a very far voyage in a ship, but Icelanders are good sailors and none of us are sick."

"Where is that, Iceland?"

He waved one hand. "Far north, where the sun stays awake all summer. But we are living in Red River Valley of Minnesota for one whole year since then. That is how I am having such good English."

"Iceland," I reported over my shoulder to Pa. "Red River Valley, Minnesota."

Pa turned around briefly. "I hear it's good farming there," he called.

Siggi's father pushed his lower lip out and shrugged. "I vas vorking on a big bonanza farm. Tousand acres veet. But too many Norvegians."

"We are making our own farm," Siggi added to the sound of the oxen's bells.

He looked proudly up at his pa, and I could tell he was aiming to run a bonanza farm of his own, someday. Word had it those giant spreads had fields bigger than some of the little states back East, with threshers pulled by forty-mule teams and hundreds of men working as hands. It seemed incredible to me, but there you have it. The West is big all over, as I well knew.

"Plan to farm wheat on your new place?" I asked Siggi.

He nodded, and suddenly another white-haired little head appeared from behind the canvas cover. Siggi took one look over his shoulder at the girl and made a horrible face. "Gunna," he said, jerking one thumb back her way. And then, "Jona," he muttered as an even smaller redheaded girl poked out.

"Hello, Gunna, hello, Jona," I hailed with a big wave. The wagon lurched in a rut and I grabbed the side of bacon. I must have taken on a wild look for a moment, because both little girls shrieked with laughter and covered their mouths with their dimply hands. At the sound, two little boys popped their heads out and peeped over their mama's shoulders. They looked just exactly alike.

"Grimur, Steini," Siggi said, sighing just the way Whitey did.

I tried not to laugh. "Are there any more?"

"Ingi is sleeping."

"Not now!" Jona giggled as a baby began to wail inside the wagon.

I scrambled back over the sacks to whisper in Pa's ear. "There's six children, Pa, except one's a baby, so maybe they only count as five. But can we ask them to stay a couple of days? Please?"

He laughed, and then clicked his tongue at the mules. "Hurry up, Whitey, we've got a party to get home to."

"Ma sure will be surprised," I said, and

then long-stepped back across the wagon again to face the Icelanders. I was feeling in my pockets and trying to keep my balance at the same time.

"I've got candies," I announced.

The sun was pretty low and fiery by this time, and when I held out my hands full of cherry suckers, they had the appearance of glowing embers with the light slanting through them.

"My name's Susie," I told them. "Do you know any games?"

Siggi nodded. "*Ja*, sure."

We gabbed all the way back to our homestead, and I was so fired up I didn't even wait for the team to stop before I jumped down from the wagon. The Eiriksson children came popping out of the wagon like crickets when you turn over a bale of hay.

"Show them where to put their stock," Pa told me, and, with a nervous smile, hurried to the door of our house.

I watched him go in and shut the door behind him, and then turned to look at my new friends. Siggi was eyeing me up and down, and I figured he was guessing he had an inch or two on me at least. The little girls were patting and kissing their oxen, and the boys were yawning and rubbing their eyes. I couldn't wait to start playing something.

Mr. Eiriksson said something to Siggi in their own language as he helped Mrs. Eiriksson, with baby Ingi, from the wagon. Siggi replied and began unhitching their steadfast cattle. "These are good oxen," he told me, unbuckling their yokes.

I stepped up to help him lift the heavy yokes from their necks. Siggi spoke to the animals in Icelandic words and we pulled them by the ears and they followed us in a pretty good-natured way over to the lean-to.

Siggi's white hair made him stand out in the dimness. "How old are you?" he asked me.

"Ten."

"I am almost eleven."

"I have a collection of eagle feathers."

"I have a new knife."

"Then let's play mumblety-peg."

We faced each other while the oxen put their muzzles in the water trough and sucked water. Siggi patted the ox nearest him and smiled at me.

I smiled back and we went outside. "Want a cherry sucker?"

He nodded, so I gave him one from my pocket. It had some lint on it, but he just rubbed it off before he put the candy in his mouth. It made a bulge in his cheek. "It's good."

We hunkered down outside the sodhouse door where the dirt was packed pretty hard. Siggi fished in his pocket for his knife, and we started playing mumblety-peg while the littler children chased each other around. The wind was still, the way it often was at sunset, and the long, long shadows of Gunna and Jona, Grimur and Steini crossed and crossed and crossed each other, arms and legs and heads all mixed up in a tangle, as though there were sixteen dancing couples in a busy reel, with their laughter and high voices like a flock of birds. Siggi was a real concentrator when it came to dropping the knife off his fingers and thumb, and when he missed, he said a word in Icelandic that I was pretty certain was a cussword.

"Ever seen a sodhouse before?" I asked.

He frowned at the knife as he set it up on his thumb knuckle. "*Ja*, sure."

"Ever been in one?"

He was still frowning, but he looked up at me from under his whitey-blond eyelashes and smiled. "No, I never been inside."

"Come on, then." I put my shoulder on the door and pushed it open, and Siggi followed me inside.

"I find it very enterprising," Pa was saying. "Moving all the way from Iceland to Minnesota and then moving again."

"Ve are making farm of our own," Mr. Eiriksson explained.

Ma was sitting at the table, as they all were, and looking at Siggi's mama and their baby, Ingi, with a look of certified amazement. "Traveling in a wagon with five children and an infant? You're a brave woman, Mrs. Eiriksson."

The woman laughed shyly and shook her head.

I crooked my finger at Siggi, and we tiptoed away from the elders and I took my box of eagle feathers off a shelf. We spread them on the floor where the light from the one west window made a stretched and golden square. "Wing feathers. Tail feathers." We touched the feathers carefully with pointing fingers, first me and then Siggi, one at a time:

the long brown feathers, some touched with gold.

"They don't come out to the prairie so often," I told him. "They're just travelers here. Just passing through."

"Like us." Siggi picked up one long, perfect feather and twirled it between his fingers, letting it brush against his cheek as it spun around. He liked them, that was plain.

I gathered them back together into the box. "You take them. It'll be a long time before you can find some of your own, seeing as how winter's coming."

He took the box with a pretty solemn nod. "Thanks." Tucking the box under his arm, he went to the table and spoke in his mama's ear. She looked at me, and then at Siggi, and she nodded. I sat on the corner of Ma's chair, and she put her arm around my shoulders, and we all watched in silence as Siggi opened the door and went out.

"You have a nice son, Mrs. Eiriksson," Ma said.

"Siggi is good boy."

"He'll be a good help to you," Ma added. Her voice got a little choked as she added, "But aren't you frightened? Starting all over again—*again*?"

Mrs. Eiriksson bounced Ingi in her arms. The baby waved her fists and stuck one in her tiny mouth. "No, it is not to be frightened. It is to be a whole new life."

"New life," Mr. Eiriksson chimed in.

Ma trembled a little. I glanced up at her, and suddenly grew fearful she was about to cry; she had such a look on her face that I didn't know what was hurting her so bad. Pa noticed it, too, because he had stopped talking to Mr. Eiriksson and was looking hard at Ma.

"Are you—" he began, leaning toward Ma with one hand outstretched.

But the door opened and Siggi came back in, carrying a wire cage in one hand. Within the cage, hopping from perch to perch, was a tiny yellow bird the color of cornmeal. Nobody said a word for a minute as he put the cage on the table. We looked at the bird, looked at its bright black eyes, its bright golden feathers and the delicate clutch of its claws. From side to side it cocked its head, blinking, looking, looking: black eyes in a yellow face.

"A canary," Ma whispered.

Siggi nodded eagerly. "Canary, *ja*. For Susie."

"Me?" I felt my mouth drop open. "It's the prettiest thing I ever saw."

"Where did you ever get it?" Ma asked.

"This canary I have hatched myself." Siggi put his face close to the cage. "I have the mama and papa birds, and this is their baby."

I put my face up to the cage, too. That

little yellow bird was the most cunning little thing, hopping back and forth from perch to perch and letting out little *cheeps* as it went. Its wings blurred in yellow flashes each time it changed its perch.

"When we live in Minnesota, Papa lives in the barracks at the bonanza farm," Siggi explained. "We live in town in a boarding-house next to the parsonage, where there lives a priest of the Catholics. His name is Father O'Hara, who is a little man with a head like an egg. All the time he raises canaries, and he is whistling to them and singing, I am thinking, because there are not so many Catholics in that town and he is lonely.

"And one day I ask to see those birds, and Father O'Hara he lets me see them. One room is all the cages of canaries, and he lets them fly around in the room. He likes them to sit on his arms and his shoulders, the little man in a black dress, and holding out his arms all covered with little birds and flying around his head in a yellow cloud.

"He says that he dreams of flying up with the canaries, that when he is reborn, he will rise up and never be sad or frightened again. I don't understand Father O'Hara when he is saying this. He is a strange man, I think. But he lets me help him with the birds, and he lets me have some and care for the eggs, and I, Siggi, am good with my hands and I make wire cages for him when he asks me.

"So I am taking my canaries west, and I am giving you one."

I looked at Siggi through the bars of the cage, past the tiny yellow bird, past its bright black eyes.

"He will sing in the morning when it is light," Siggi said, putting one finger through the bars to touch the feathers.

Ma stood up. She was staring at Siggi. "How do you know? How can you be so sure?" Everyone looked at her, nobody spoke. "He may have been happy and brave at home, but now he's out here. How can something so small sing out here where it is so big?"

"He is not too small," Mrs. Eiriksson said.

"*Ja*, that's true," Siggi agreed, nodding his head fast. "Sometimes it is the littlest ones have the best voice, missus."

I was looking up at Ma, and she stared at the canary as though she expected some powerful example of magic from it. The little yellow bird hopped from perch to perch, tipping its head, fluttering its wings. Nothing happened.

Ma's shoulders sort of sagged and she turned away from the table. "Come, Mrs. Eiriksson," she said. "I'm sure the children must be hungry."

THREE

They made ready to leave the next morning while it was still dark. The birdy voices of the little children as Mr. and Mrs. Eiriksson lifted them from their blankets, and Siggi's voice cracked with sleep, and Pa talking quietly about the road to take woke me up. I saw Ma at the stove making coffee and clutching a blanket at her throat.

I shuffled into my shoes and a jacket and followed Siggi outside. "Thanks for the canary," I said again. "Are you sure it'll sing?"

"*Ja,* sure." He adjusted a buckle on the

harness by the light of a lantern. Our breath fogged in the little circle of light, and a cloud steamed up from the oxen's noses.

I raised the lantern from the ground to give him more light. "Too bad you have to move on today."

Mrs. Eiriksson was settling the young ones in the wagon, and she laughed softly at something Jona said. Then she spoke gentle words in Icelandic, which I didn't understand, of course, but I was sure they were words like "darling girl, your mama loves you, go to sleep now," and I felt my chest squeeze tight.

"I wish you didn't have to leave today," I said.

Siggi stepped around me to reach the second ox, his solemn attention on his work. "My mama and papa are very happy to be finding our new place, very much in a hurry."

Then he looked up at me with a bright white smile. "It is like being born new, like Father O'Hara said."

"You said he was a strange man," I said with a certain grouch in my voice.

"Doesn't mean he was wrong."

Suddenly it was time for them to leave, Pa and Mr. Eiriksson shaking hands and Mrs. Eiriksson going back inside to thank my ma, and the oxen catching the stir in the air and shifting their big weight from one hoof to the other, and then Mrs. Eiriksson back outside and climbing up onto the seat and ducking into the wagon to speak to the little children.

"Good-bye," Siggi said to me.

"Good journey." I held my hand out, which seemed like the correct thing to do, and he shook it.

Pa came to my side and we watched Siggi and Mr. Eiriksson climb up and call to the oxen, and the wagon set forth with a jerk. It was only the faintest light, still, and the wagon was gray in the grayness, and grew dimmer and fainter as it moved away, until one minute it was there like a ghost and the next minute it was gone in the dark west. Pa and I stood side by side not saying anything and not moving. But I wanted to say something, or do something. I couldn't credit that the day would now be like the other days, that these voyagers could come and leave and we not be changed. They had been an example of some way of facing the wide world that I was determined to benefit from.

"Ma wouldn't come out to see them off," I said.

"No, she wouldn't," Pa replied.

The gray was lifting and lightening, and I knew the colors would start soon and the sun rise. I took a glance behind me to the east. Then I ran to the door and pulled it wide open, and the sleepy canary in its cage on the table fluttered its yellow wings in fright.

"Ma!"

She was folding blankets, her head bowed. "Yes."

"Ma, come up on the roof with me."

She raised her head at that. "Susie, I'm not—"

"Ma, please," I begged, taking her hand and pulling all my weight against it.

Ma staggered a little to gain her balance, and looked down at me, frowning. "Why?"

"I want to show you something." I seized the advantage and began dragging her to the door. Through it I could see the paleness of the east. We passed Pa, and Ma shook her head as though to say, "I don't know."

She stopped in her tracks, even though I tried dragging her forward. She hadn't stepped much past the doorway in a long time, and I could tell she was reluctant to take another step.

"You've got to, Ma."

She hesitated another moment, and then

stepped toward me, and then took another step, faltering and unsteady as a baby, and bit by bit I dragged her around the corner of the house to where we could climb up onto the roof.

"Up here?" she asked, squinting up, full of uncertainty.

"It's easy as anything," I promised. "Hurry."

And with me going first and reaching back to help her, we got up onto the roof and stood there in the cool breeze and faced the east. The horizon had a red edge, one long furrow from one end of the earth to the other.

Ma hugged her arms around herself, and her dress and apron pressed against her legs and her hair flew back in wisps.

"Susie, what is this? I want to go back inside."

"No, Ma, wait, don't go in, please."

She shivered, and hugged herself tighter. "I don't like it up here, it's too big."

"No, it's not, it's not too big." I took both her hands and pulled her arms apart, pointing her arms north and south. "Like this, Ma. Stand like this."

We faced the east, and the sky grew pink and gold, and the colors went spreading out between our arms, an armful of the bravest, fiercest, strongest light, and the round red eye of the sun opened on the horizon and the sky filled with brightness. The light came straight over the prairie from the edge of the world to where we stood, and hit the sodhouse, hit our faces, hit the open door below us.

And from inside the house came the sweetest singing there ever was, like an angel waking up and being glad. The sunshine grew stronger, and the birdsong grew louder and gladder, and I saw a tear on Ma's cheek that sparkled like crystal in the new light. I didn't hardly dare breathe, I hardly *could* breathe, and Pa, standing on the

ground below us, looking up like he couldn't hardly breathe either. Ma stood in the breeze with her arms reached forward, with the sun rising up on her fingertips and the canary's song reaching out to the sun like it came from her fingertips. We all stood without speaking a word while Ma made the sun rise and turned the prairie to gold and the sky to blue.

Then she turned to me with a smile, smiling at me and holding out her hand and saying, "Good morning, Black-Eyed Susan."

I put my face in her apron and hugged hard. And I decided I'd ask later if she would make a pie.

ABOUT THE AUTHOR

Jennifer Armstrong is the author of many highly praised books for young readers including *Chin Yu Min and the Ginger Cat, King Crow,* and the novel *Steal Away.* She lives in Saratoga Springs, New York.

28 Days

DATE DUE

JUN 19 '96		
JUL 17 96		
APR 10 '97		
MAY 3 97		
SEP 03 '97		

Juvenile FICTION
Armstrong, Jennifer, 1961-
Black-eyed Susan

DATE

28 Days

Juvenile FICTION
Armstrong, Jennifer, 1961-
Black-eyed Susan